BLACK BEAUTY

BLACK BEAUTY

Anna Sewell

Om KIDZ
An imprint of Om Books International

Reprinted in 2018

Om
KIDZ | Om Books International

Corporate & Editorial Office
A-12, Sector 64, Noida 201 301
Uttar Pradesh, India
Phone: +91 120 477 4100
Email: editorial@ombooks.com
Website: www.ombooksinternational.com

Sales Office
107, Ansari Road, Darya Ganj
New Delhi 110 002, India
Phone: +91 11 4000 9000
Fax: +91 11 2327 8091
Email: sales@ombooks.com
Website: www.ombooks.com

© Om Books International 2013

Adapted by Hitesh Iplani

ISBN: 978-93-82607-02-1

Printed in India

10 9 8 7 6 5 4

Contents

Chapter One

My First Home

The first thing I remember from my younger years is a big sloping meadow and a pond with water lilies at the deep end. There were green trees that bent over the pond. We would go there when the weather was warm. In winters, we would stay in a warm shed nearby.

Most of my time was spent with my mother, galloping in the meadow with her or resting under the shade of a tree. At night, I would lay down by her side. I used to drink my mother's milk then, since I was too young to eat grass.

I loved frolicking with the other young horses in the field. There were six of them and I was the youngest of them all. We would run around a lot and sometimes we would kick and bite each other playfully.

Then one day, when we were all at play, my mother called me over to her. When I went to her, she said, "I hope that one day you will grow up to become a good horse. Be gentle and hardworking, and do not bite or kick others even if you are just playing." I would remember her advice forever.

My mother was a wise horse. Her name was Duchess. Our master, Farmer Grey loved her a lot too and affectionately called her 'Pet'. He gave us good food and cared for us as if we were his own children. Even old Daniel, the man who was in charge of looking after the horses, was very gentle. We were very lucky.

We loved Farmer Grey very much. My mother would whicker with happiness and run up to him whenever she saw him standing at the gate. He

would then gently pat her nose and say "Hey sweet Pet, how is little Blackie doing?"

He called me 'Blackie' because of my coat, which was of a dull black colour. Although all the other horses also came up to him, I think we were his favourites. He would always go to the town on market day with my mother pulling the carriage.

A young boy named Dick used to come to the meadow to pluck blackberries from the tree. After having his fill, he would start throwing stones at the colts for fun. It might have been fun for him but we colts would get bruised and hurt.

Once, Farmer Grey was close by and Dick was completely unaware of his presence. As always, after eating the blackberries, Dick started throwing stones at us. Seeing this, our master was livid with rage. He caught the boy by his arm and slapped him so hard that the boy started yelling in pain.

"You are quite a mean fellow, aren't you, hurting innocent animals like that!" Farmer Grey growled at him. "This is bad! And it may not be the first time that you have done this but it is most definitely the last time you hurt my animals. If I see you on my farm again, I will beat you black and blue!" And that was the last time we saw the boy.

Chapter Two

Breaking In

I was growing up to be a good-looking horse. I had an elegant, deep black coat with one white foot and a white star on my forehead. Everyone admired the way I was turning out to be. Farmer Grey, however, did not want to sell me till I was four years old. He said it was not right for young boys to work like men and for colts to work like adult horses.

When I turned four, Squire Gordon came to take a look at me. I walked, trotted and galloped for him. He then checked my eyes, mouth and legs and said that once I had been broken in I would make a fine horse.

Farmer Grey decided to break me in himself. He did not want me to be frightened or to get hurt in the process. He told Gordon that he would begin the very next day.

In a horse's world, to 'break in' means to train a horse to wear a saddle and bridle, and to carry a rider on its back. A horse must also be trained to pull a cart. He must be able to adjust his speed according to the driver's desire.

A good horse must stay calm at all times and never act on an impulse, throwing the rider off balance. He must always do what his master asks him to. He should not bite or kick other horses. And the most important, and hardest of all requirements, is that when the harness is on, he must not jump or lie down.

I had been wearing a halter and a headpiece for some time, so I was quite used to them. A headpiece is that part of the bridle which fits around a horse's head. Now, I was to have a bit and a bridle. The bit is a piece of metal held

in the horse's mouth by reins and is used to control the horse while riding. The bit is inserted into a horse's mouth between the mouth and over the tongue. The ends of the metal piece come out at the corners of the mouth and are tied to straps. These straps go over the head, under the throat around the nose and under the chin, helping the rider control the horse.

That day, Farmer Grey fed me some oats as he did every day. Now, the bit causes a lot of pain. So, Farmer Grey had to encourage me by gently caressing and talking to me to get the bit into my mouth. After that, the bridle was put in place. It took me some time and a good amount of oats to get used to the bit and the bridle.

After that, he put a saddle on my back very slowly. During the process, old Daniel held my head gently. This happened every day after that. Farmer Grey would come and put the saddle on my back, then he would pat me, talk to me in a soothing voice and feed me oats. Gradually, I began to look forward to these meetings with the master.

One morning, something very unusual happened. After saddling me, Farmer Grey climbed on to my back and rode me around the field. It felt quite strange, nevertheless, I was quite happy and proud to carry my master around.

At that point I believed my 'breaking-in' was complete. But contrary to what I thought, it was far from over. There was more to come. I only found out when I was taken to the blacksmith. I was to be fitted with iron shoes.

Farmer Grey made sure that I was not hurt or scared during the process. First, the blacksmith clipped off a little from each of my hooves. It was done so gently that I did not feel any discomfort. Then he fitted a piece of metal, shaped like my foot on each of my feet. To make sure that the shoes didn't come off once I started to trot, the blacksmith nailed them to my hooves thoroughly and carefully. It did not hurt much but it did feel quite rigid and heavy initially.

After the shoes, I was made to wear the harness. A harness is an arrangement of leather straps used to attach a horse to the cart. I was also fitted with blinkers for my eyes. They fit so snugly to the sides of my eyes, that when they were on, I could only see what was straight in front of me. Blinkers make sure the horse wearing them can focus only on the path straight ahead, with no distraction.

My saddle was also fitted with a crupper — a thin leather strap that is attached to the saddle so as to prevent it from slipping forward. The strap went right under my tail. It was very uncomfortable. I felt like kicking, but I loved and respected my master too much to do that.

I was then sent to another meadow that was close to the railway tracks, and I was to stay there for two weeks. My experience with the train was quite frightening. I would run away as fast as I could every time I heard a train coming. However, I soon realised that these dark, shrill beasts, which is how they seemed to me, would always stay on the track and would never come near us. Also, they came and went so frequently that I soon got used to them.

Since then, I have come across many horses that run fanatically or throw their riders every time a train passes by. But thanks to the time I spent near the trains, I am always calm and composed at railway stations or a crossing.

I also learnt a lot from my mother. Farmer Grey would often put me and my mother together in a carriage. My mother was an experienced horse. She was always calm and composed. She told me that if I behaved properly I would be treated well. She also told me that it was always better to try and please my master. She cautioned me that not all men were tender and considerate. They were some who were mean and would often try to hurt you.

Another thing that she told me got me very upset about my future. She told me that I could

not choose my owner. Right now I was lucky to have a caring master like Farmer Grey, but someday in life I might have to work under a merciless or foolish owner. I was worried. What did my future hold?

Chapter Three

Birtwick Park

It was in early May that Farmer Grey finally decided to sell me to Squire Gordon. He patted me softly on my back and said "Goodbye Blackie!" I was heartbroken to leave the place I had until now called home. The squire took me to a place called Birtwick Park which was to be my new home.

Squire Gordon's home was a large country house. I was kept in a stable with four stalls. It had a large window which swung open into the courtyard. I was not tied in my stall and could move freely. This made me very happy. The place was clean and well-kept. The walls around the stable were not very high and I could easily see what was happening in the yard.

After relishing my first meal in my new home, I found out that my neighbour was a plump, grey pony with a thick coat and tail. He had a rather interesting nose. I looked over the wall and said, "Hey! What's your name?" he took one look at me and then just rattled on, "I am Merrylegs. Everyone likes me. Mostly I carry young women on my back, but at times I also take our mistress out in the low carriage. I'm quite good-looking, don't you think? Are you my new neighbour?" When I replied I was, Merrylegs said, "I hope that you are a good horse and do not bite or kick me."

I noticed another horse looking over its stall and watching us. She was a chestnut coloured mare and her ears were laid back against her head. She looked angry and did not answer when I tried to talk to her. Her name was Ginger, as I later got to know from Merrylegs.

When in the afternoon Ginger went out, Merrylegs told me that she was called so because she was in the habit of snapping at everyone. Ginger's previous owners had been very cruel to her because of which she had developed a bad temper. Merrylegs said that he had noticed gradual improvement in Ginger's behaviour, and the reason for that change was the good treatment she had received since she came here. John, who was the groom here, was quite gentle with her. Merrylegs had absolute faith in John's care.

Chapter Four

Freedom

Even though I was quite happy in my new home, I missed the carefree freedom of Farmer Grey's farm. For more than three years that I spent at my first home, I had been allowed to roam freely in the meadow. At Birtwick Park however, things were very different. Here, I had to stay in my stall all the time, until there was some work for me. Even during work I had to stand steady and obey my new master's commands.

I was riddled with straps all around me, a bit in my mouth and blinkers covering my eyes. It was very difficult for me since I was young — my

body filled with the strength and spirit of youth. I was used to running at full speed, tossing up my head and flinging my tail freely. It was quite hard living the life of a working horse.

John was a very experienced groom. It showed in the way he handled the horses. Sometimes, when John came to take me out for a run, I was so full of energy that I could hardly be steady. But John would let me run as fast as I could whenever we were out of the village.

On Sundays, the horses were let free in the fields to roam. The grass felt soft and cool to our iron-clad hooves and it was wonderful to be able to walk and run freely. Even a small amount of freedom on the field made up for the rest of the week.

Chapter Five

Ginger

I had a chance to talk to Ginger when, one day, we were standing alone in the shade. I told her all about my first master, my mother and my breaking in. "I wish I had a master like yours. And a good home like yours where they treat horses nicely. Now, it is too late to change the way I am."

I asked Ginger why she thought so. She told me that she had been separated from her mother when she was very young. There was no one who would take care of her and look after her. No one showed her any affection. In the field where they moved about, a boy would throw stones at the colts. Even though Ginger never really got hurt, another young horse got hit on the face so hard that he had to carry a scar all his life. It was a terrifying experience for her. Her breaking-in was horrifying as well. Some brutal men forcibly fitted the halter and the bit into her mouth, and flogged her when she protested.

That was not all. Ginger was put in a dark, dingy stall which was too small for her. Her master's son, who was breaking her in, was cruel and insensitive. He would stay drunk all day long and whenever Ginger disobeyed him, he would make her run around the field until she was too tired to even stand. One day, he made her run so long and hard that she got exhausted and fell sick.

He came in early next morning and started riding her around the field without a break. Ginger was already tired and when she started slowing down, he came down heavily upon her, hitting her with his whip. It was more than she

could take and she started kicking and jumping without thinking. Eventually, as soon as she managed to throw that brute off her, she ran away without looking behind.

For quite some time, she wandered in the fields. With no food or water, her condition deteriorating with every passing day. She became weak and flies buzzed around her head in the hot sun. Then one day, as the sun set, a benevolent old man came up to her and fed her oats and gave her fresh water to drink. He took her back to the stable with gentle and encouraging words, but he did not hurt her in any way.

He then washed her injuries with warm water and gently caressed her while she rested. She was then given another trainer called Job. He was very kind and caring. He taught her all that was expected out of her.

Chapter Six

Ginger's Story Continued

The next time we met, Ginger told me about her second home. She was bought by a fashionable gentleman living in the city. He only cared about how he appeared to others. He wanted everybody to take notice whenever his carriage rode by. He would keep Ginger's reins pulled very tight for long hours at a stretch to keep her head held high. She was made to wear two bits which would chaff at her tongue so much that it would bleed at times.

Whenever she had to wait for her master outside, she was not allowed to move even a single muscle. She was whipped whenever she tried to rest her head. If she protested in some way, she was whipped again. She was never spoken to kindly by anyone. All this made her miserable and angry all the time. She would get angry at anyone who came close to the harness. She feared everyone was trying to hurt her in some way.

She said she wanted to be a good, hardworking horse and make her owners happy. But she was never given the right treatment and encouragement.

At last, she broke out of her harness and ran away. She became angry and ill-tempered. Nobody wanted to keep her. She was sold off as soon as the owner would realise that it was impossible to train her.

Before she arrived at Squire Gordon's place, her owner handled her roughly and would jab at her with a pitchfork if she got unruly. One day, he tried to flog her with a whip. Ginger could not

take it anymore and she bit his hand. After that he was scared to come too close to her. Ginger took this to be an important lesson in dealing with human cruelty. By biting and kicking people she could evade it.

"However, since I've come to Birtwick Park," Ginger said, "My life has changed in many ways. John and James, the stable boys, treat me very nicely." I was glad that it was so, and I noticed that as time passed she became more and more happy and sweet tempered. She was no longer the angry Ginger of my first day.

Chapter Seven

Merrylegs

Mr. Bloomfield, the vicar, had a large family with many children. They would often accompany him to Birtwick Park as they really liked riding around on Merrylegs.

One afternoon, when James brought Merrylegs back to the stable, he said, "You should learn to behave yourself otherwise we will get into trouble." Merrylegs had been out with the children for quite some time. I asked him what the problem was.

"It's those kids! I have taught them a fine lesson now. They just don't understand that I too get tired! So I threw them off my back!" I was quite shocked at hearing this, especially from Merrylegs, who loved children. I couldn't believe that he could do such a thing. He was very gentle with them otherwise.

When I asked him why he had behaved like this, he told me that they had been riding him for more than two hours and they had wanted to ride even more! Since he was slowing down with exhaustion, they had made whips out of hazel sticks and had hit him hard. Merrylegs explained that he had stopped a few times to indicate that he was tired. But the boys were being insensitive and cruel. They refused to understand that even he could get tired. When one of the kids whipped him on his legs, Merrylegs simply could not endure it any longer. He had kicked back with his hind legs and thrown the boy off his back.

After he had narrated the whole incident, Merrylegs turned to me and said, "You know Blackie, I would never have done something like

this had those kids not troubled me so much. I don't like kicking people or showing bad temper. If I did, Squire Gordon would definitely sell me at the town market. And who knows who my next owner might be. I might be forced to work till death at some butcher's shop or may be brutally flogged by cruel men for no reason. "

Chapter Eight

A Talk in the Orchard

The grooms would often let us out to graze in the orchard. Once, on a warm and sunny day, we were grazing in the shade. I stood next to Sir Oliver. Sir Oliver was an old but very handsome horse. His tail, curiously, was only five or six inches long and had a tuft of hair sticking out from it. I had always wanted to ask him about the tail.

"It was no accident!" he grumbled when I finally asked him. "It was done intentionally and it was a cruel act! Those who did it should have been ashamed of themselves. I was taken to a very bad place when I was young. They tied me up and cut off my tail. I couldn't even move. They cut through the flesh and the bone. That was a day spent in absolute agony."

I was shocked. "It must have been dreadful!" I cried.

"It was. But what was even more dreadful was the humiliation I suffered. It was an essential part of my body! With my tail gone, I cannot even brush away the flies. Now, I can never have it back and nothing can replace my tail."

"But why! Why did they cut it off?" Ginger enquired. I wanted to ask the same question too. "It was all for fashion! Can you believe that? Ridiculous!" Sir Oliver replied and stomped his foot on the ground in anger. "Some idiot must have thought that horses looked better with short tails. Somebody should have told the man that if horses were intended to have short tails then God would have made them that way."

"People can go to any extent to stay in fashion. They don't even spare dogs. They cut dogs' tails, pin back their ears, only because men think that it makes them look more attractive. I had a very close dog friend. Her name was Sky and she used to sleep in my stall. She had a litter of five puppies.

One day, a man took her puppies away. When they did not return for a long time, Sky had to go out to find them. When she brought them back it was a pitiable sight. A part of their tails had been cut off. The puppies were bleeding and crying. Even their ear flaps were sheared off. Poor Sky! She had to lick their wounds all night to stop them from crying."

Remembering the sad incident overwhelmed Sir Oliver. He stopped speaking and gave out a long sigh. I waited quietly for him to finish. I really wanted to know what happened to the puppies.

"Their wounds healed," Sir Oliver began again, "but they never forgot the pain. It's funny but these people don't cut their own children's ears or their noses or any other part. Why do they do this to us animals?"

Sir Oliver was a gentle horse. But after narrating the incident, he was very angry. This happened whenever he spoke about man's obsession with looks and fashion. I too felt angry. Ginger went ahead and declared that men were brutes and complete morons.

"That is a bad word, Ginger!" said Merrylegs approaching us. He had been scratching himself against the apple tree. "What are you talking about, and Ginger, why did you use that word?" Merrrylegs asked.

Ginger replied that bad words were meant for bad things and she had used the word "moron" to describe certain human beings who were inconsiderate and cruel towards animals.

Then she told him all about Sir Oliver's tail and Sky's pups.

"Well, I have seen that happening to dogs a couple of times myself," Merrylegs said, "but we live in a nice place. People here do not treat us cruelly. So let us not talk about it here. We should be happy that we are at Birtwick Park."

Merrylegs was right. Whatever he said made us happy again and aware of our present. All this talk had made us hungry, so we focussed on eating the sweet apples.

Chapter Nine

A Stormy Day

I had been at Birtwick Park for quite some time. One day, Squire Gordon came to my stall. He gazed at me intently and gently patted me on my head. Then he called the grooms and asked them how they liked the name "Black Beauty".

"It is a fine name, Sir, and it suits him perfectly!" said John enthusiastically. Even I puffed up on hearing such a majestic name. After naming me, my master asked John to put me before the dogcart. My master had to make a trip into town for business. I was happy that I was put before the dogcart. It had rained a lot the previous night and there was a strong wind blowing. A dogcart is light and its high wheels run very smoothly on mud tracks. So we travelled with good speed up to the wooden bridge over the river.

As soon as we reached the bridge, a man came hurrying towards us. "The river is rising rather rapidly," he said, "It is going to be a rough night!" Many meadows were already submerged under water. At some places on the road, the water almost reached my knees. However, my master was an experienced rider so he drove on very carefully.

We reached town safe and sound, although, I felt tired after the journey. I guess it was because of the rough weather. But since my master's work took a long time to finish, I rested for quite some time before we started for home in the late afternoon. By that time, the wind was picking up again and it was getting much stronger than before. The master told John that he had never been out in such a terrible weather. As we

moved ahead, small branches started breaking apart from the trees because of the strong wind.

My master told James that it would be best for them to get out of the woods as soon as possible lest one of the branches fall on them. John agreed and he increased the pace a little.

We had not gone much further when a huge oak tree fell down right in front of us. It had been torn right from the roots. "That was a close shave!" exclaimed my master. "What are we going to do now?" John replied that it was not possible to go over or around the tree and it would be better if we went back to the wooden bridge.

When we reached the wooden bridge, it was already dark. Water had risen over the middle of the bridge. But James did not stop assuming it was just flood water. However, the moment I put my foot on the bridge, I knew something was not right. I stopped right there and refused to move ahead.

My master gave me a gentle tap with his whip asking me to move on. Then he hit me a little hard. But I still refused to move.

John figured I must be scared so he jumped off the cart and came over to me. He took the reins in his hands and tried to pull me forward. "Come on, Beauty! Don't be scared! The bridge is right there!" he said.

I wished I could tell him that something was not right with the bridge. I could feel it. I knew that if I moved ahead I would land all of us in danger. Just then the gatekeeper, who had moved away to a nearby shelter because of the storm, came out running towards us. "Hey! Don't cross the bridge! Stop!" he screamed.

"Why, what's wrong?" my master asked. "The flood has washed away a part of the bridge in the middle. It is broken. Had you crossed, you'd have landed straight into the river and would have been washed away. Not a soul

would have known where you had gone!" the gatekeeper replied.

My master and John stood there, aghast. The next thing I knew, they were patting and gently stroking me admiringly, clearly astonished by the fact that I could sense danger, which no one else could even imagine. And although I had no idea as to why I did not want to move ahead and why I felt the way I did, couldn't help but feel proud having saved these men who cared so much for me. We bid farewell to the gatekeeper and took another route back home.

By now the wind had died down a little. However, it had grown pitch dark. The woods had an eerie feel about them. I moved along quietly. I could hear my master and John talk. "Man may have the power of reason by his side, but it's the animals that are still in touch with nature," John agreed and recounted many instances of animals saving their owners from

danger. They both agreed that people did not value their animals enough.

It was almost midnight when we reached Birtwick Park. The gardener was waiting for us at the gates. He told us that the lady of the house was still awake and was waiting for us inside the house. However, hearing the sound of the cart she came running out to meet us.

"Oh! Are you all right? I was worried that you'd had an accident on the way. It is such bad weather," she said. "No, sweetheart, we did not have an accident. But we might have been drowned in the river had it not been for our dear Black Beauty here," my master replied.

The mistress gently patted me and whispered a thank you in my ear. They went inside and John took me to the stable. He made a delicious meal that night and laid extra straw on my bed. I was glad. It had been a long and tiring day.

Chapter Ten

James Howard

One early morning in December, the master came to the stable. He had a letter in his hand. John was just getting me back into the stable after my morning exercise.

"Good Morning, John," said Master. "What do you think about James? Have you had any complaints about him?" The inquiry sounded rather serious.

"James is an honest man, Sir. He is hard-working and is good to the horses," said John, surprised by this sudden question.

My master looked pleased on hearing this. He smiled and turned to look at James who was standing in the doorway.

"James, come here! I was asking John about you because what I am about to tell you bears heavily on your future. My brother-in-law has a written to me asking for a young groom who is honest and loyal. Needless to say, he should be well acquainted with his tasks. And I think there can be no better person than you. My brother-in-law is a good man. I stand to lose a talented and trustworthy man, James, but I do not want to deprive you of an excellent opportunity. Think about it and let me know."

After a few days, James agreed to work for the master's brother-in-law. It was then decided that James be given a good deal of driving practice before he joined his new place of work. Ginger and I were harnessed to the carriage. And we, along with James, drove all around the city. While James got his practice, we enjoyed visiting

a new place every day. It was the first time in my life I had seen so many horses and their carriages. The whole city seemed to be moving at the same time.

Chapter Eleven

The Fire

One morning, my master and mistress had to visit some people who lived about forty-five miles away from Birtwick Park. James, by now, had become quite good at driving the carriage over long distances, thanks to his daily practice runs. He knew how to handle Ginger and me rather well, and was able to cover thirty-two miles on the first day. The journey included climbing up some rather steep hills. But James maneuvered us so well that Ginger and I didn't feel any discomfort at all.

We stopped twice on the way, to get some rest. By the time the sun set, we had reached the town where we were supposed to spend the night. We were staying at a large inn located in the centre of the marketplace. The entrance of the inn opened into a large yard. When we reached inside, two men came to us. One of them patted me and led me to a stall in the stable. Ginger was taken to another stall by the other man. The grooms of the inn cleaned us up and James stood by all the while to keep an eye.

I had been resting a while in the stall, when I noticed a young man, with a pipe in his mouth, talking to the grooms. One of the grooms told him to put out his pipe and lay some straw on a horse's bed. The man passed by me to throw some hay. After finishing his task he left and locked the door.

Sometime in the middle of the night, I woke up with a start. Something did not feel right. It was dark and I could not see anything. I was finding it very hard to breathe for some reason. I could hear Ginger coughing and other horses

were restless too. After a while, when I got used to the dark, I realised that the stable was filled with smoke.

I could hear the gentle sound of crackling and snapping. The sound sent shivers down my spine. I knew what that sound meant. All the horses were awake now. They were growing restless and were trying to break loose from their halters.

The air was getting too thick to breathe now. Just then, one of the grooms hastily opened the door, carrying a lantern in his hand. He was scared and his hands were shaking with fear. He had come in to let the horses loose and move them out. But he fumbled with the knots and the horses too refused to move. They were all affected by his fear, including me. He even tried to forcibly pull me out but I was too strong for him. Eventually, he gave up and ran outside.

The gust of fresh air that came with the opening of the door did us good but only for a short while. The sound of crackling was getting louder, and I could see a red light shimmering on the wall.

It was then that I heard someone shout, "Fire!" then suddenly, out of nowhere, James called out to me in his usual cheerful and soothing voice, "Come, my dear, Beauty, it's time to go."

I was the one closest to the door so he carefully pulled me along with him, gently urging me to move. Soon, we were out of the burning stable. It was safe in the yard so James handed me over to someone else and went back into the stable to get Ginger. I was afraid that something might happen to him and out of fear I let out a whimper. Later on, Ginger told me that my whimper had saved her life. Had she not heard my voice that night, she would not have been able to leave the stable.

After that, all hell broke loose in the yard. Other horses were being let out of the stable

now. People ran helter-skelter, shouting and screaming at each other. Ignoring all the mess, I focused on the stable door. A lot of smoke was coming out of that door.

Nothing seemed to be moving when I heard my master's voice calling out James: "James! James Howard! Where are you?"

Nobody answered to my master's call. However, there was a loud crash and as if in response to his call, James came out of the stable holding Ginger's reins and coughing badly. I neighed with joy and relief at seeing them. The master too was relieved to see them safe.

My master went over to him and gently patted him on the shoulder. "You were quite courageous tonight, James! Are you all right?"

James merely nodded his head. He was unable to speak for quite some time after that.

My master decided to leave the town that very night. Everyone looked quite disturbed by

the incident. Later, during the journey, James revealed that the roof and the floor of the stable had caught fire and had fallen. The horses that could not, get out got buried there.

Chapter Twelve

James Leaves Birtwick Park

Fortunately, we did not face any more such disasters through the rest of our journey and reached our destination well before sunset. We were taken into a comfortable and clean stable. A kind-hearted coachman took care of us, and when he heard about the fire and James' courageous act, he applauded him.

The coachman told James that his horses really trusted him, otherwise, it is next to impossible to get horses out of a stable in case of a fire or a flood.

After a three-day stay at that place, we returned to Birtwick Park. The journey back was uninterrupted, except we still felt uneasy about the fire. Ginger and I couldn't stop thinking about all the poor horses that had to pay with their lives for a human's carelessness.

The sight of our own stable raised our spirits. John was very happy to see us, and even more happy to find us safe and unhurt when he heard about the incident. John later told James about a young boy named Joe Green. Joe was to be James' substitute. John said that at fourteen years the boy may be young but he was hardworking and very eager to learn.

Joe Green came to Birtwick Park the very next day. James told him all that he was supposed to do at the stables every day. James taught him how to sweep the stable and how to put out the straw and hay. Joe wasn't tall enough to groom either Ginger or me, so James started training him on Merrylegs. Initially, Merrylegs was not very happy about being handled by a young

boy, but soon he realised that Joe was learning fast and was going to be fine by the time James finished with him.

Time flew by and soon the day came when James was supposed to leave us. The air seemed to be filled with sadness that day. Everyone, including the mistress, was sad that James was leaving. Even James, who tried his best to act cheerful, looked sad. He told John that he was going to miss his family, his friends here and the horses whom he loved so much. John told him not to worry as his friends and family were quite happy for him. This was a once-in-a-lifetime opportunity for him and he ought to take it.

After James left, Merrylegs stopped eating and remained sullen for days. John had to take him out to the field and let him loose for a while. The fresh air and good exercise improved Merrylegs' mood. But we all still missed James who was not only a good groom but also genuinely cared for us.

Chapter Thirteen

Going For the Doctor

One night, I was sleeping in my stall when I heard a loud bell. And then I heard John's door being thrown open and his footsteps on the floor as he ran across the hall. Suddenly, the stable door flung open and John hurriedly came over to me. He woke me up and said, "Black Beauty, tonight you will have to run like you have never run before."

Quickly, he placed the saddle on my back and the bridle on my head and took me to the hall door. The butler was standing there holding a lamp.

"Go John! Don't waste a minute! Hand over this note to Dr. White and do let the horse rest a bit at the inn. Come back as soon as you can!"

As soon as we reached the road, John said to me, "Do your best. We have to save the mistress' life, Black Beauty."

I could sense that something was wrong. There was a note of urgency in John's voice. For nearly two miles I ran as fast as I could. At the bridge, John pulled me up a little and said, "Well done, Black Beauty!"

I knew John would have let me go slower but I was too excited. Before John could urge me further, I was running swiftly again.

We reached the doctor's house at three o'clock in the morning. John had to bang his fists on the door to get it opened since nobody had answered the door even after he rang the bell twice. After what must have felt like an earthquake to the doctor, he opened a window and asked John what the matter was. John told him that the mistress

was not doing well at all and that the master had sent a note for him.

When the doctor read the note he told him that he must hurry. The doctor's own horse was ill so he had to ride back with me. John knew that it would be a little too hard on me for I was overworked and tired. But he had no other option.

The doctor was an old man and he was not a good rider. I had to make up for his bad horsemanship. When we reached Birtwick Park, Joe was waiting for us at the gate. My master came out and took the doctor inside. Joe took me to the stable. It was good to be home after such a difficult night. I was tired and my whole body was shaking. I was sweating heavily and my body was overheated. Joe put some extra straw on my bed and fed me hay and corn. He also gave me some cold water. But he forgot all about covering me up in a warm blanket.

Satisfied with all that he had done for me, Joe closed the door and left. After some time, I started feeling cold. My whole body started shivering and I wished that I had my warm blanket on me. Had John been here, he would have been smart enough to put the blanket on me. I missed John who must have still been walking home from the doctor's house. My whole body was aching and my legs and chest felt sore.

After a while, I heard the stable door open. In a moment I found John by my side. He must have returned form the doctor's place and must have heard me moaning. Immediately, he covered me with warm blankets. "Joe is so stupid!" he said. He was angry at Joe for not covering me up and not feeding me something warm.

I was sick. I had developed a strong fever and there was inflammation in my lungs. It was hard for me to breathe. John was by my side all the time, giving me my medicine on time and feeding me properly. My master came to see me almost every day. John told him that he had never seen

a horse run so fast. My master gently stroked on my neck and said "Thank you, Black Beauty."

My whole body was in pain and I could barely stand out of weakness, yet I felt proud and happy that I had helped in saving my mistress's life.

It took me some time to get better. The doctor came to see me many times. John remained angry with Joe Green for quite some time. But he realised later that Joe did not do it on purpose. He told Joe to be much more careful and that he needed to spend more time at the stable to learn about horses.

Chapter Fourteen

Leaving Birtwick Park

For about three years I had lived quite happily at Birtwick Park. However after our mistress fell sick, I had a feeling that something sad was in the offing. Our mistress could not completely recover after that. The doctor kept coming to the house, sometimes rather frequently even in a single week. Our master appeared worried and anxious all the time.

One day, finally, the doctor told our master that moving to a warmer climate for some years might help the mistress. Soon, my master decided to move and told the servants to start packing for the long trip. Everyone was sad and shocked to hear this.

John did his usual work, but he talked little and barely smiled. He looked tense too.

This was the beginning of an end to our stay at Birtwick Park. We were all going to be separated. Ginger and I were sold to an old trusted friend of the masters. Merrylegs was sold to a local priest on the condition that he would never sell Merrylegs.

The day my master and the mistress were to leave, Ginger and I brought the carriage to the hall door for the last time. When all the arrangements were done, my master brought the mistress down the steps carrying her in her arms. He bid farewell to all the servants and appreciated them for their service.

We drove slowly to the railway station. When we reached the station, my mistress said to John, "Goodbye John! We will always miss you!"

John did not reply but I could feel a gentle tug in the reins. Joe pulled the bags out of the carriage. John asked Joe to stand by the horses and he himself went to the platform with the master and the mistress. Joe was crying too.

Soon the train came and Master boarded along with his wife. Doors were closed and the guard signalled. Slowly, the train vanished into clouds of white steam. Our hearts were saddened by his departure and the uncertain and disruptive prospects of the future.

John came out after sometime. "They are gone," he said without any hint of emotion in his voice.

He and Joe climbed up the carriage and we quietly drove back to the house.

Chapter Fifteen

Our New Home

Our new home was called the Earlshall Park. Joe came up to us next morning to say goodbye. Merrylegs whickered to us from his stall. John put the saddle on Ginger and put me in the lead and we rode to our new home.

At Earlshall Park, John asked to see Mr. York. We waited a good time for the man outside. After sometime, an elegant-looking gentleman came out and greeted John in a friendly and polite manner. Then in a stern voice he ordered a groom to take us to the stable.

The groom put us in a stable full of light and air and put us in stalls beside each other.

Sometime later, John and Mr. York came to the stable. Mr. York asked John about our habits, tastes and dislikes. John told Mr. York that we were a good team, and if treated properly we would be excellent performers. He also told Mr. York about the hardships Ginger had to go through. He warned Mr. York that if treated badly she could turn bad tempered again.

Before leaving the stable John said, "We have never used a check-rein with either of them. Ginger had developed her bad temper because of the gag-bit that she was forced to wear." A check-rein is used to hold the horse's head high. It does not allow the horse to lower its head. A gag-bit, too, is a similar kind of device. Both these device cause much pain to the horse.

Mr. York replied in his stern voice, "John, I'm afraid the horses will have to wear a check-rain. I myself like a loose rein. The owner is kind to horses. But his wife wants that the horses be reined tightly according to latest fashion. "Sir",

said John, "these horses have always been treated nicely at Birtwick Park. They will do well if they are treated well!" he pleaded.

John then turned to us. I lowered my head to hear his soothing and sad voice. I so wished then that he would stay but I knew it could never be so. He said goodbye and was soon gone. We never met again.

The man who had purchased us came to the stable next morning. He seemed quite impressed with us. Mr. York started telling him about all that John had told him. He also told him about the check-rein. But the man disapprovingly shook his head and said that it was out of his control. The man's wife demanded a tight rein on her horses. However, he assured Mr. York that he would allow us sufficient time to make us comfortable to the check-rein.

Next morning, the new owner's wife came to take a look at us. She was tall and was dressed elegantly. She did not make any comment as she observed us. We were put before the carriage after we were harnessed. She got into the carriage and we started riding.

It was for the first time that I was wearing a check-rein. It was uncomfortable as I could not lower my head even once. But it wasn't very bad as it did not pull my head higher than I was used to. Initially, I was a little concerned about Ginger. But she did not say anything and did not appear at all troubled.

This happened the next day too. We were harnessed and put on the carriage. Our mistress came down to take a ride and told Mr. York that he must pull the horses' heads higher. She said she wanted us to look elegant.

Mr. York tried very hard to convince her otherwise but she did not pay any attention to his requests.

That day, I was reminded of all the stories I had heard about the cruelty of masters. And it dawned upon me later in life that the way we

were treated at Birtwick Park was quite special and rare. Our reins were further shortened every day. I began to be scared of the very thing I had loved most in my life until then. The harness now became a symbol of pain. The most difficult part was pulling the carriage up a hill. I could not lower my head, and my back and my legs would ache badly. Ginger too was disturbed but she did not say anything.

The rein remained at a particular length for quite some days. I started thinking that the worst was over. But now, as I recall the events that happened after that, I realise I could not even have imagined the tortures that were yet to be inflicted upon us.

Chapter Sixteen

Rebellion

One day, the lady of the house came a little late for her ride. She ordered Mr. York to lift our heads up higher than usual and seemed furious about something. I was the first one whose head Mr. York held back and set the rein. It was unbearably tight and very uncomfortable. Ginger was aware of what was to come. So, when Mr. York went to Ginger, she began to twitch and move her head right and left. In the very next moment, just as soon as he took hold of the rein to adjust it, Ginger reared up, hitting Mr. York in the nose. Also, the groom standing close to him practically lost his balance.

Ginger was uncontrollable. No matter what they did to calm her, she only grumbled and kicked more. Her movements kept becoming more frantic until she slipped after hitting the carriage pole. Mr. York took this opportunity, and held down Ginger's head to keep her from battling further.

I followed the groom back to the stable after he set me free. Soon Ginger also came accompanied by two grooms. There were marks and bruises on her body. When Mr. York came to see her, he seemed angry at first but then I noticed a hint of sadness in his expression. I heard him say to the grooms that it was not right to treat horses in this inhuman manner only to satisfy a woman's fancy.

Ginger was very lucky since as soon as her bruises healed, she was taken by the master's son on a hunting expedition and she was not put on the carriage again. However, now a new

horse accompanied me since I was still to remain a carriage horse.

The check-rein caused many problems. For four long months, I could not breathe properly because of the weight it put on my wind pipe. My mouth now foamed occasionally because of the abnormal angle of my head during a ride. It was not uncommon for the sharp edges to bite on my tongue as well as my jaw. With every passing day, I became more unhappy and dispirited.

I had no well-wishers at Earlshall Park. Everybody was callous and cruel to us. Mr. York knew that we were in pain, but he dared not disobey the master and the mistress.

Chapter Seventeen

Reuben Smith

The stables were taken care of by a man called Reuben Smith when Mr. York was not around. Although Mr. Reuben was a gentle man and knew how to take care of horses, he was not very dependable. This was because he drank a lot of alcohol. There were times when he was completely sober and then other times when he drank alcohol excessively. During such episodes, he was unkind to his wife and troublesome to his neighbours. It was Mr. York's wish that Mr. Reuben must not consume any alcohol as long as he was working at the stables.

It was the month of April and the family was to arrive home in May. So that Reuben could run errands, I was picked to pull the carriage. He drove the carriage to the town at a decent pace. I was taken to rest and eat food once we had reached the town. The stable groom did not observe that a nail in one of my front shoes had loosened. Some hours later, Reuben returned to inform the groom that we would not be going back for another hour since Reuben had met some old friends. By now the groom had noticed the nail and had cautioned Reuben. Reuben however ignored his warning.

"It will be alright until we get home," he said rather rudely to the boy.

It was rare for Reuben to be so unconcerned about me or the carriage. Normally, Reuben was careful with his job and kept the horses healthy and fit.

It was nine o'clock when Reuben came back for the journey back home. He had spent hardly

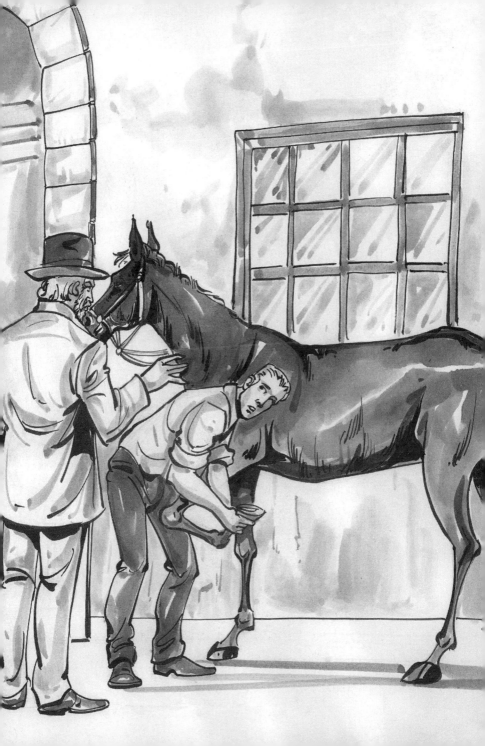

an hour with his old friends. We started our journey in the dark and even before we had exited the town, Reuben started to run me in a gallop. Because the stony road and fast speed the nail, which was already loose, came off and the shoe fell. Reuben pushed me to run faster. He had not noticed that my shoe had dropped off because he was completely drunk. Soon, my hoof broke and I saw how badly the inside was cut because of the sharp-edged stones.

Since we were travelling at a very fast pace, I fell with immense pressure on my knees. Reuben had fallen off my back and lay groaning a few steps away. Quickly, I regained my balance and realised that I was in tremendous pain. Oddly, at that very moment, I started to think about the wonderful times when my mother and I would roam blissfully in the lush green meadow.

As time passed, the pain in my foot grew worse. These memories helped to distract me from the pain. I was concentrating hard,

straining for a hint of the sound of footsteps, wishing and hoping all the time for someone to come and help us.

Chapter Eighteen

How It Ended

It was dark and late when I suddenly heard the sound of horses' feet approaching us. As the sound drew closer, I was sure that it was Ginger. I neighed as loud as I could to draw their attention. To my great relief, the carriage came and stopped at seeing a figure lying unconscious on the stony road.

A man jumped out of the carriage, held Reuben's arm and soon after declared him dead. "Feel how cold his hands are," he said.

Another man came down to help him and together they tried to see if Reuben could stand or walk. It was when the moonlight hit his face that we realised his hair was drenched in blood. After they laid Reuben down, the men saw how badly I was injured in both knees and foot. It did not take them very long to understand that Reuben's drinking had led to this accident.

They talked to each other for some time and then we started a mournful journey back home. Once I reached the stable I was taken care of. My knees were covered with wet cloth and my foot bandaged with ointments. Although it was acutely uncomfortable, I managed to lie down on straw and drown into a deep slumber.

A doctor came to see me the very next day. He said there was a strong chance that my wounds would heal completely, however, the marks from the wounds would always remain. The process of healing was slow and agonising. They did all they could to cure me. When the scar tissue grew in my knee, they burned it with the help of ointments and medicines. They put a biting

solution on both knees to take the hair off, once the wound had fully healed.

An investigation into the sudden death of Reuben was held. The town innkeeper informed the authorities that Reuben was extremely drunk when he left the inn the night of his death. The groom added that he had seen a loose nail in my shoe. The shoe that had been tossed among the stones had been found by someone. Therefore, how the sudden accident in which Reuben lost his life had occurred, was clear to everyone.

Chapter Nineteen

Ruined and Going Downhill

Soon my knees got better and I was let into a small meadow. I grazed there alone. I loved the freedom and the green grass but felt rather lonely. I missed Ginger very much. We had become good friends. I would try to talk to the horses passing by the meadow on the road but they rarely replied.

One day, as I sat missing Ginger, I heard someone approach. I turned around to take a look at the visitor. It took me a moment to realise that it was really Ginger walking towards me! I was surprised and happy to see her. She said that she was sent here to keep me company. With all the hard riding she had been made to do, her body and spirits were in a bad shape.

We both had changed a lot from what we used to be in our early days. Nevertheless, we were still happy to be back together. We did not run or prance in the field, but just grazed and silently stood under the shady trees.

A few days after Ginger arrived at the meadow, the master came to examine us with Mr. York. He had come back from a long trip and he seemed anxious.

"I haven't lived up to my friend's expectations," he said. "He trusted me with them. Let Ginger stay here for some time. She needs rest. However, I must sell him. His knees are not going to heal," he said, pointing towards me.

Mr. York recommended a man he knew. He told Master my condition would not be a problem for him and the man was kind.

My master agreed and soon I was sent to this man by train. The man, to whom I was sent, put

me in a comfortable but small stable. He owned many horses and carriages which he offered for hire. Sometimes, his own men would drive the carriage and sometimes the people who hired it drove themselves.

I had been driven by skilled drivers before. Now, all sorts of drivers drove me. Once, there was a man who hired me and on the way he lashed hard at me with the whip, even though I was keeping a fine speed. The road was full of stones and a stone got struck in my front hoof. The man did not even notice it. He was busy enjoying himself.

It was only after we had covered a considerable distance that he noticed that I was limping. A kind farmer stopped us and took the stone out of my hoof. Even though I was put on hire as a task horse, I was ill-treated and wounded by many other people like this one.

However, I was once hired by an experienced gentleman who knew all about riding horses. He

was nice and kind to me. I was glad to be at his service. Soon I was galloping at my best speed. This raised my spirits significantly.

The man liked me a lot. He wanted to buy me for a friend of his, who wanted a gentle horse for riding. My master agreed and soon I was sent to my new master, Mr. Barry.

Chapter Twenty

A Thief

Mr. Barry was a businessman and the house in which he lived was small. His doctor had told him that horseback riding would do his health good, and thus, he had rented a stable. He also hired a man named Filcher, as my groom. Although Mr. Barry had very little knowledge of horses, his behaviour with me was very nice. For food, I was fed the best hay mixed with lots of bran, crushed beans and oat.

Soon, I became used to my new routine and began to enjoy this calm life. The groom kept the stable in order and washed me regularly.

One day, however, I noticed that something was wrong with my food. There were very little oats in the food that I was being given. I grew upset and rather weak because of this, but I knew that there was no way I could tell my master.

It was when Mr. Barry once rode with me to the countryside to meet his friends, that the question of my weakness was raised.

"Your horse does not look well," his friend said. "He seems malnourished."

Mr. Barry was puzzled and told his friend that he was feeding me the best food. After pondering on the matter for a while, Mr. Barry came to the conclusion that someone must be meddling with the food.

At that moment, I really wished I could talk, because, then I would have told Mr. Barry that every morning, Filcher would bring along with him a little boy, who always carried a tiny, covered basket. They would go to the harness room, fill a bag with oats, and hide it in the basket. The

groom's theft, however, was soon brought to light. Like every day, the boy left the stable. However, as soon as the boy shut the door, a constable pushed it open and stood there holding the boy. The boy tried to call out to Filcher since he was very scared. The constable, however, made him show where the oats were.

A lot of crying and quarrelling ensued after which the boy told the constable that Filcher was involved in this. Finally, they were both put behind bars. Whereas the boy was released, I later found out, Filcher remained in prison.

Chapter Twenty One

A Horse Fair

Filcher's replacement was not a good groom either. He was careless and lazy. For days, he would not clean my stable and seldom exercised me. I had to live in a damp and untidy stable due to which I developed an infection in one of my hooves.

Mr. Barry thought he had had enough. Both his grooms had disappointed him bitterly and caused him great loss. So he decided to put me on sale at a horse fair.

At the fair, I was made to stand with good-looking, strong horses. The fair was full of people of all ages. They would take a look at us and leave. Some came to enjoy the hustle-bustle. For the rest—including the horses—it was all business.

A serious buyer would always check a horse thoroughly. First, he would pull open a horse's mouth. Then he would check its eyes, moving on to the rest of the body. Some people were crude and insensitive, while some were gentle and soft-spoken.

Then came a man who looked rather kind. His soothing and gentle voice reminded me of all the good masters I'd had before. He was short but sturdy and had gray eyes.

He offered to buy me and named a good price for me. Unfortunately, he was refused and in his place a rough-looking man with a booming voice asked about me. Thanks to my lucky stars, he did not offer to buy me. However, he returned after a short while and started negotiating my price. I was scared again. At that very moment, the man with gray eyes returned and as if I was asking him

for help, I extended my head towards him. The man offered more money than the rough looking man and bought me.

My new master quickly took me out of the fair and fed me oats. He chatted with me for a little while before we started for my new home.

We rode for a long time and reached a small house. My master got down and whistled. The door of the house burst open and a young woman followed by a little girl and a boy ran out. They greeted my master and welcomed me.

The master then described the fair to his family. The children kept patting me and speaking to me gently. They made me feel as if they had known me all my life. I felt happy and peaceful after a long time.

Chapter Twenty Two

A City Cab Horse

The name of my new master was Jeremiah Barker. His friends called him Jerry. My mistress' name was Polly. The little girl was called Dolly and the little boy, Harry. Dolly was eight years old and Harry was twelve. My mistress was a pretty woman with dark smooth hair, black eyes and a sweet little mouth. It was a close-knit family and they loved each other very much. Jerry used to drive a cab in the city. I, along with his other horse Captain, was to pull the carriage.

On my first day, Polly and Dolly came to the stable to see me. They were very friendly to me. It was after such a long time that I was being given such affection. They fed me apples and some bread. They said that I was very good-looking and wondered what had happened to my knees.

Jerry put me into the cab for the first time in the afternoon. He made sure that the collar and the bridle were comfortably fitted. No check-rein was put on me and I could move my head with ease. Jerry was very happy to have me and he bragged about me to other cab drivers. Many cab drivers were doubtful that something must be wrong with me since I was a good-looking horse. Jerry just smiled in answer every time someone said that.

For the first week, pulling a cab gave me a tough time. I was not used to the noises of the city and the crowded streets. But I trusted Jerry and I gradually got used to my job.

Soon, Jerry and I had developed a deep understanding of each other. Not only was he a good and kind master, but he also had tremendous

knowledge about horses. He kept our stables clean and fed us properly. Sunday would always be a day of rest for us. It was the best thing about being a cab horse. There was no work to be done on Sundays. We would unwind and talk to each other leisurely. Captain immediately accepted me as a friend. I had started to love my new home.

Chapter Twenty Three

Jerry Barker

Jerry turned out to be one of the best masters I'd ever had. He had complete faith in himself and he always asserted what he believed in. He never picked up a quarrel with anyone. Jerry did not like wasting time and was very punctual. It really angered him when people whipped their horses to run faster because they themselves were late.

One day, two young, crazy-looking men called Jerry and said, "Look here, cabby! We are running late and we have to catch the one o'clock train. If you can get us to the station on time, we will reward you with double fare."

Jerry told them that he would drive at the normal speed and would charge only what was due. The two men were in a hurry so they hopped on to the carriage quickly.

It is always difficult to drive in the city during the day. The streets are crowded with people and carriages. But it takes the team of a good driver and a good horse to surprise their passengers. Jerry knew the streets well. We drove so smartly through the crowded streets that we arrived at the station five minutes before one o'clock.

The two men were really relieved to have made it in time. They thanked Jerry and me, and offered to pay extra money to Jerry. But as he had said before, he only took what was due and returned the extra money. Jerry helped them with their baggage and soon they disappeared in the crowd. Jerry was wondering why the men were in such a hurry since there would be another train in a short while.

Later on, after we returned home, Jerry fed me oats and cleaned me and told his family about the two young men and how he and the horses skillfully drove through the traffic and dropped them at the station five minutes before time. The family had a good time imagining funny reasons for the young men's haste.

Chapter Twenty Four

Poor Ginger

One afternoon our cab was waiting, like the rest, outside the city park. A dirty old cab came and stood by ours. An old, tired-looking chestnut mare was pulling it. The chestnut's coat was dull and her bones were jutting out of the skin. Her legs were weak and shaking. I was eating some hay when some of it got caught in the wind and flew towards her. The pitiable animal extended her long, weak neck and picked it up. She seemed hungry. I noticed her eyes and she looked familiar to me.

"Is that you, Black Beauty?" she asked. I knew that voice! It was definitely Ginger. But the horse that stood in front of me was not even remotely close to the Ginger of old times. Her neck was now sunken in and her coat had lost its sheen. Her body was wounded and sore. I could tell that she had been through a lot. Pain and suffering was clearly visible on her face.

I was shocked to see her like this and could not say anything. She understood and came closer to me.

She told me that after spending twelve months in the field where I had left her, she was considered fit to work again and was sold to a new owner. She seemed to do fine initially but the extra effort damaged her muscles. She was sold and resold again and again.

Eventually, she was sold to a man who rented cabs and horses. The passengers would soon find out about her weakness and would pay less for her. She was deployed on a smaller cab.

There too, the passengers or the rider would whip her for going slow. "They never cared for the condition I was in. I did not even get Sunday rest," she said.

"But you were not one to take it silently. You were famous for your bad temper once," I said.

"That was a mistake. Humans are stronger than horses. All you can do is keep waiting for your time. There is no use protesting. If you have cruel owners, it's your bad luck. I wish I could die now. Only that can put an end to all my miseries."

I gently touched my nose with her's. There was no need for words. Before she left, she told me that I was the only friend she had. She must have been happy to see me.

Her driver pulled her out of the cab line and drove off. After a short while, I saw a cart carrying a dead horse pass by. Its head was hanging out of the cart and blood dripped off its tongue. I saw the white streak running

down its forehead. I wished that it was Ginger. That was the only way she could have escaped her troubles.

Chapter Twenty Five

Jerry's New Year

Holidays might appear to be great times for most of the people but they are not so for cab drivers and their horses. They have to stand in frost or rain, waiting for their passengers, shivering with cold. All this time, their passengers are busy dancing and celebrating in big, warm houses.

So, just like the other city cabs, we too had a lot of work. And even though Jerry was suffering from a bad cough, he still went out to work even late in the night. However, no matter how late we reached home, Polly was always waiting for us. She would come carrying a lantern in her hand, worried about Jerry's health.

A day before the New Year, two gentlemen hired us to take them to a house in the city square. When we dropped them, they told us to return again at eleven and wait for them. It was nine o'clock then.

At exactly eleven o'clock, we reached the door. We waited there for almost an hour but nobody came out.

It was a cold night and the wind was sharp. Jerry put one of the blankets on my neck to save me from the cold. But he was in a bad shape. He had been coughing for quite some time. There was no shelter nearby where we could have protected ourselves from the cold.

About fifteen minutes after one o'clock, the door opened and the two gentlemen came out chatting merrily. They gave Jerry the address and told him to drive fast. I could barely feel my legs because of the cold and I would have fallen

had I not resolved to be strong. The gentlemen did not apologise for keeping us waiting for so long. To top it all, they were mad at Jerry because they had to pay him extra for the delay.

Jerry kept coughing all the way back home and even when we had reached home, he was still coughing. Polly was clearly worried but she did not say anything. Before Jerry ate, he gave us food and a massage.

Next day, there was no sign of Jerry. His son came to the stable to clean us and feed us. I figured something was wrong. Polly too came to the stable to tell her children that their father was very ill.

We waited anxiously for Jerry's health to improve. After a week or so, Polly declared that Jerry was now out of danger. Jerry got better but the doctor said that Jerry could not drive the cab anymore.

Even though his health was improving, Jerry remained bed-ridden for a long time. It was during this time that Polly and he received a letter from an old widow who was a family friend. She offered them a cottage near her home. She said that there was a good school for the children close-by.

Jerry decided to move to the country as soon as he was better again. It was obvious that the horses and the carriage would be sold. The effect of age was now visible in me. Nobody would want an old horse. I was very sad to hear this. It was after such a long time that I had a good master to work for and such a loving family around me. And though my work was hard, a good master made it possible for me to like it and do it well.

Jerry did not want to sell me for cab work, so he asked his friend to find a good home for me, where they would treat me right. Jerry had been prescribed bed-rest by the doctor so I never got to see him again. The children and Polly came to the stable see me off. They wanted to

take me with them but said they were helpless. They looked sad. Polly gently stroked my neck and kissed me. I could feel the gentle touch of her hand even when I was far away from them.

Chapter Twenty Six

Jakes and the Old Woman

I had been sold to a man who knew how to take care of horses and had a moderately big house. He was a baker and a dealer in corn. Even though my new master was a good man and was good to me, his servants, were not the best ones. He was barely there to see what they were doing. The foreman of the stable was always intent on making everyone work more and more. He was always in a hurry. In his bid to finish as much work as possible, he would often overload me with cargo. My driver, Jakes, was an experienced man and he cautioned him many times. But the foreman never really paid any attention to him.

I was made to wear a check-rein again. After four months of overloading and hard work, my body began to fail me. Once, while climbing a steep road, I completely lost my strength and could not move. The driver, Jakes, got angry and started shouting at me.

I tried but could not move. Jakes warned that if I did not move he would whip me. Before I knew it, he started hitting me with his whip. The hard leather bit into my flesh. I was about to give up and fall, when I heard a woman's voice asking Jakes to not to hurt me more. She said that if he could loosen the rein a little, I might be able to pull through.

I was fortunate that Jakes listened to her and loosened the rein. This gave me some relief and I lowered my head and pulled the cart up the road. The woman came closer to me. She was an old woman. She gently brushed my neck and told Jakes that a check-rein is not good for a horse and it made it difficult for them to pull a heavy cart.

Jakes consented and took off the check-rein. But the overloading still continued. Not realising that I was ageing and becoming weaker with every passing day, I was made to pull an overladen cart.

My miseries did not end here. After work, I was put in a stable where there was almost no light. I lost my eyesight faster than I would have otherwise. I became even more sad and alone.

Chapter Twenty Seven

Hard Times

Soon, I became too weak to work and was sold. My new master's name was Nicholas Skinner. He was a mean looking man with a hooked nose. I would often think he looked like a vulture. He never smiled and always wore a stern expression. His voice was rough and it sounded like the noise of cart wheels over a gravel path.

After I started working for Nicholas Skinner, I came to know what real misery and pain meant. All my previous hardships seemed nothing compared to what I had to go through under Skinner. He owned a fleet of old, dirty-looking cabs. What was even worse was that they were driven by very bad drivers. Skinner was hard on everybody. The horses had to bear the double brunt of Skinner and his men. There was no Sunday rest, and the work duration was long even in hot weather.

Many Sunday mornings, I would have to take some men out to the country. They would force the driver to take them up and down hills with sharp slopes. When we would get back from these crazy rides, I would be too tired to even eat. I remembered the cool barn mash that Jerry made for me during summer. Often, I thought of how good it was at Jerry's. The good meal and the Sunday rests made it possible for me to work in the summer heat. Here there was none of that and the situation was unbearable.

My driver was even more terrible than Skinner. His whip had a sharp iron piece at the end. Every time he hit me, I would bleed and that happened a lot. My entire body bore the marks of

his cruelty. This driver would hit me on my head and my belly. Only I knew how much pain I was in. I missed Jerry and his family immensely. Here, I was made to work like a machine. My owners wanted to make me pay for my every breath.

They did not care if any of the horses died, since we were anyway old and worn out. My condition reminded me of Ginger. I too wished that death would come and rescue me. One day, it almost happened. I had been at the stand from eight in the morning and was already tired by the time it was noon. Then, I dropped a man at the station where a family of four came and asked my driver if he could take them to the town. They had a lot of heavy luggage and when they were finished loading, the younger daughter of the man took a look at me and told her father that I looked rickety and old. She said, "Papa he is too weak to carry us and the luggage!"

The father too expressed his doubts to the driver. But the driver was too eager to prove to them that I was strong enough to carry them and also the luggage. The cab creaked under all the weight.

I had not been fed since morning, and I had been working all day. I still tried to do my best. We were going fine until we came across a raised section of the road. I pulled as hard as I could. The driver kept throwing his whip at me. All of a sudden, because of the intense pain the whip caused, I lost control and slipped. I was too weak to move or even open my eyes. Angry voices and the sounds of luggage unloading came as if from somewhere far away. I could not make sense of what was happening around me. Just then, I heard a sweet voice say, "I told you he would not be able to take it, Papa! This is our fault. Help him!"

Then somebody loosened my bridle and took off the collar. "I think he is dead. He won't be able to get up again," I heard somebody say. Then I think a policeman, seeing the commotion, must

have arrived there as I could hear orders being given to clear out the space and bring me some water and blankets. I still could not open my eyes. I could barely breathe. Somebody threw some cold water on my head and poured some down my throat also. A blanket was put over me and I lay there for what seemed like a long time.

Finally, after some time I started to gain my senses and slowly lifted my head. A kind-looking man was sitting beside me, gently stroking me and encouraging me to get up. With some help, I was able to stand on my feet. I was slowly led into a nearby stable. I was given a comfortable stall and some warm food.

After spending the entire night at that stall, I was finally strong enough to be taken back to Skinner's stable. He came to check on me next morning. "This horse cannot take it anymore," he said. "With some good amount of rest he might be able to work again. But I cannot deal with that. I cannot afford to nurse sick horses."

He decided to give me a ten-day rest and then sell me at a horse fair. He wanted to get the best price out of me, so, for those ten days, he gave me good food. But even that could not help me regain my health. I still looked weak and worn out.

Chapter Twenty Eight

Farmer Thoroughgood and His Grandson

Due to my poor frame and old age, I was put along with all the worn out horses. Some were old, some weak and some looked so thoroughly exploited and ill that it would have been kind to kill them.

The buyers and sellers looked alike. The buyers were poor men trying to buy a horse at the cheapest price possible, and the sellers were rough men selling almost useless horse at the highest price possible. Humanity was reduced to its basest form and I was sad to be in such a place, where it was not possible to trust anyone.

However, I noticed a man wearing a broad hat. He had a strong built with round shoulders and a broad back. He looked like a farmer. There was a hint of kindness in his face and his eyes. I looked at him and tried to catch his attention. There was a young boy by his side.

"Look here, Willie! That horse has known better days I can tell you that," he said to the boy. "He must have been a beauty to look at in his youth."

He extended his hand and gently touched me on my neck. I responded by putting out my nose. The boy caressed my face and said, "You are right, Grandpa. He must have been something. Poor horse! He responds to kindness. I think you can get him to be his old self again, Grandpa. What do you say? You did with Ladybird."

The farmer replied to his grandson that Ladybird was not old but only tired and abused.

But the boy liked me and asserted that I too just needed good people to recover.

The farmer smiled and touched my sore and swollen legs. Then he took a look inside my mouth and decided to buy me. The deal was settled quickly with whatever few dollars he offered.

They both then took me to their home and the grandfather entrusted the boy with my care. The boy fed me a lot of hay and oats daily and took good care of me. During daytime, he would let me roam in the meadow freely. He even brought carrots sometimes and spent almost all his time with me.

With such good care and love, I regained my health fast. My wounds healed and my legs got better. Soon, I was able to pull the carriage and take them to town. They seemed happy with my improvement and decided that it was time to let me go to a good home where I would be taken care of and loved.

Chapter Twenty Nine

My Last Home

One summer morning, the groom paid extra attention to my cleaning and brushing. I sensed that something new was going to happen. Both the grandfather and the grandson seemed excited as they got into the carriage.

"I'm sure the women will admire him," said the grandfather. "If they do, they will be glad to have him. And the horse too will have a good home."

We drove for a mile and arrived at a small house with a garden in the front. Three elderly women came out of the house and welcomed us.

One of the women, Miss Ellen instantly liked me and asked many questions about me. They were told that I had been exploited and abused, but now, if I was treated with love and kindness I would turn out to be a fine horse.

The women wanted to try me out before they bought me. Willie hugged me and the farmer gently patted me before leaving.

I was taken into a stable and was fed a good meal by the groom. When he was checking me he noticed the star on my forehead. "That is strange!" he said. "The star is quite similar to the one Black Beauty had! And he is about the same height as Black Beauty too!"

He quickly ran his hand over my neck and found what he was looking for. It was a mark that was left by and injection that had been given to me when I was young. He seemed excited and in doubt at the same time.

"This seems too good to be true," he said. "Black Beauty had the same star on his forehead.

His right foot was white and he had a small patch of white on his back. And this horse has exactly the same markings. It must be him! It must be Black Beauty!" he shouted.

I was confused who this man was and why he was talking to himself like that and how come he knew my name. Then he said to me, "Black Beauty! Don't you remember me? I'm Joe, Joe Green, from Birtwick Park! I worked under John and almost killed you when I did not put a blanket over you in that cold weather. I was a little boy then."

And then it all came back to me. Of course it was Joe! I was quite happy to see him after so many years. We both joyfully looked at each other. Joe would not stop caressing me and asking me how I had been. I wished I could tell him. From the next day onwards, Miss Ellen and her sisters took me out every day. They started to like me as much as I liked being back with Joe.

Now, it's been almost a year and I'm very happy. Joe is very nice to me and takes good care of me. With every passing day, my strength is returning to me. The farmer and his grandson often visit me. The women have decided to keep me forever. I find it hard to believe that my bad days have finally come to an end. At last, I am at home.

About the Author

■ Anna Sewell

Anna Sewell (30 March 1820 – 25 April 1878) was an English novelist. She was best known for her classic novel *Black Beauty*.

Sewell was born in Norfolk, England, into a devoutly Quaker family. Her mother, Mary Wright Sewell (1798–1884) was a successful author of children's books. She had one sibling, a younger brother, named Philip. They were educated at home.

When Anna was fourteen, she slipped while walking home from school and severely injured both of her ankles. Her father took a job in Brighton in 1836, in the hope that the climate there would help to cure her. Despite this, and most likely because of mistreatment of her injury, for the rest of her life Anna was unable to stand without a crutch or to walk for any length of time. For greater mobility, she frequently used horse-drawn carriages, which contributed to her love of horses and concern for the humane treatment of animals.

While seeking to improve her health in Europe, Sewell encountered various writers, artists, and philosophers, to which her previous background had not exposed her.

Sewell's only published work was *Black Beauty*, written during 1871 to 1877, after she had moved to Old Catton, a village near Norfolk. During this time her health was declining. She was often so weak that she was confined to her bed and writing was a challenge. She dictated the text to her mother and from 1876 began to write on slips of paper which her mother then transcribed.

Sewell sold the novel to local publisher on 24 November 1877, when she was 57 years of age. Although it is now considered a children's classic, she originally wrote it for those who worked with horses. She said "a special aim [was] to induce kindness, sympathy, and an understanding treatment of horses".

Sewell died on 25 April 1878, five months after her book was published, living long enough to see its initial success.

■ Characters

Black Beauty: The protagonist of the novel. He was given the name 'Blackie' or 'Black Beauty' because of his dull black colour. He had a star shaped mark on his forehead. He was a good, loyal, hardworking horse who served many masters sincerely, even when some mistreated him.

Duchess: The mother of Black Beauty, who instilled values of loyalty and hard work in him.

Farmer Grey: Master of Duchess and Black Beauty. He was a kind and caring master, who was heartbroken when he had to sell Black Beauty.

Squire Gordon: The owner of Birtwick Park. He bought Black Beauty from Farmer Grey, as a carriage horse. He was a kind, caring and rewarding master. He was concerned about his horses, and acknowledged their contributions or achievements. He was forced to sell his farm, to move to a warmer place.

Merrylegs: A plump, grey pony who was the first horse Black Beauty met at Birtwick Park. He was very proud of his looks, and was a gentle horse. He didn't pull any carriages, but carried the mistress around the estate and he was very proud of that fact.

Ginger A chestnut coloured mare, who did not trust easily. She became a very good friend to Black Beauty eventually. She did not trust people very easily, as she was exploited and mistreated by many owners. Squire Gordon was the only master she has, who treated her lovingly and really cared for her.

John: The experienced, caring groom at Birtwick Park. He genuinely cared for all the horses.

James Howard: Another groom at Birtwick Park, who was a gifted groom and very hardworking. He saved Ginger and Black Beauty from a fire in the stable. He left Birtwick Park after he got a better job prospect.

Joe Green: When he joined Birtwick Park, he was a very young man. He was hard working but not experienced. Due to his fault, Black Beauty fell sick. Black Beauty met Joe Green again, unlike John or James. He worked for Miss Ellen, who was the last owner of Black Beauty.

Mr. York: The owner of Earshall Park. Even though he understood that he was exploiting his horses to fulfil his wife's whims, he did not do anything to help them.

Ruben Smith: The irresponsible groom, because of whom Black Beauty injured himself severely.

Mr. Barry: A rich businessman, who is kind to the horses, but sells them as soon as he realised that they are incurring too much cost.

Jeremiah or Jerry Barker: The cab driver, who is an honest man and loved Black Beauty. He took care of him, but had to sell him when they were forced to move away.

Nickolas Skinner: The mean owner, who inflicted a lot of pain on Black Beauty. He never cared for his failing health or injuries.

Farmer Thoroughbred: The farmer who bought Black Beauty. His grandson took complete care of Black beauty, and restored him back to his health.

Miss Ellen: The last owner of Black Beauty. She and her sisters took great care of Black Beauty.

■ Questions

Chapter 1
- *Who was Farmer Grey's favourite horse? What nickname did he give that horse?*
- *What are the values Duchess spoke about to Black Beauty?*
- *Was Farmer Grey a caring master? Site an incident to support your claim.*

Chapter 2
- *Explain the term 'breaking-in'.*
- *What are the various accessories a carriage horse is meant to wear?*
- *Where was Black Beauty sent for further training and why?*

Chapter 3
- *Who was the first horse Black Beauty met at Birtwick Park?*
- *Describe the nature of Merrylegs.*

Chapter 4
- *What does Black Beauty mean by 'freedom'?*
- *Who is John?*

Chapter 5
- *What kind of mistreatment did Ginger have to endure at the hands of her first master?*

Chapter 6
- *Was Ginger's second master any better than the first one? How did he treat Ginger?*
- *What kind of mistreatment did Ginger endure, before she reached Birtwick Park?*

Chapter 7
- *What mischief did Merrylegs do to be reprimanded by James?*
- *Why did a gentle horse do any mischief with the vicar's children?*

Chapter 8
- *Who is Sir Oliver? Why was his tail chopped off in half?*

- *Were Sir Oliver's previous owners nice people? Explain.*
- *What word did Ginger use to describe 'people'? Did everyone agree with her?*

Chapter 9
- *Why did Black Beauty refuse to get on the flooded bridge?*
- *What was the explanation that John gave for Black Beauty's behaviour at the bridge?*

Chapter 10
- *Why did Squire Gordon enquire about James from John? What did John reply?*
- *Who were the two horses to be chosen for James's training?*
- *Why was Black Beauty happy to help James in his training?*

Chapter 11
- *What woke Black Beauty up at night?*
- *Was James successful in saving Ginger from the fire in the stables?*

Chapter 12
- *Who joined Birtwick Park, in place of James?*
- *Why did everyone miss James after he left?*

Chapter 13
- *Why was Black Beauty woken up at the middle of the night by John?*
- *Was the Doctor a good rider?*
- *What did Joe Green do after Black Beauty came back to Birtwick Park? What did he forget to do?*
- *Who took care of Black Beauty when he fell ill?*
- *Why did John forgive Joe Green for his mistake?*

Chapter 14
- *Why did Squire Gordon have to leave Birtwick Park?*
- *Who bought Merrylegs? Under what condition was he sold?*

Chapter 15
- *What was the name of Black Beauty's new home? What was the name of his new master?*

- What did the master insist that the horses would have to wear? Was Black Beauty or Ginger happy about it?

Chapter 16
- Why did Ginger refuse to wear check-rein? What did she do to prevent it?
- Why did Ginger have marks and bruises on her body?

Chapter 17
- Who was Ruben Smith?
- What did Ruben Smith not notice, which could have prevented the accident?

Chapter 18
- What was the extent of Black Beauty's injury? Would it heal?
- What did people discover from the sudden investigation of Ruben's death?

Chapter 19
- Was Mr. York guilty for his behaviour towards Black Beauty and Ginger?
- Why was Black Beauty sold off?

Chapter 20
- Who were the thieves? What did they steal?
- Were the thieves caught? What happened to them?

Chapter 21
- Why did Mr. Barry decide to sell Black Beauty?
- Where was Black Beauty taken to for sale?

Chapter 22
- What was the name of Black Beauty's new owner? What was his occupation?

Chapter 23
- Why were the customers very angry at Jerry Barker?

Chapter 24
- *What did Ginger think was better than living in the conditions they were in? Did Black Beauty agree with him?*
- *What did Black Beauty wish for Ginger?*

Chapter 25
- *What was the reason for Jerry's illness?*
- *Why did Jerry sell Black Beauty?*

Chapter 26
- *How was Black Beauty exploited by the new owner?*
- *How did the old woman help Black Beauty?*

Chapter 27
- *Who was the new owner of Black Beauty?*
- *Why did Black Beauty fall down while pulling the cab?*

Chapter 28
- *Who bought Black Beauty?*
- *Who took care of Black Beauty and restored his health?*

Chapter 29
- *Who was Black Beauty reunited with? Was he happy to see him?*
- *Who were the last owners of Black Beauty?*